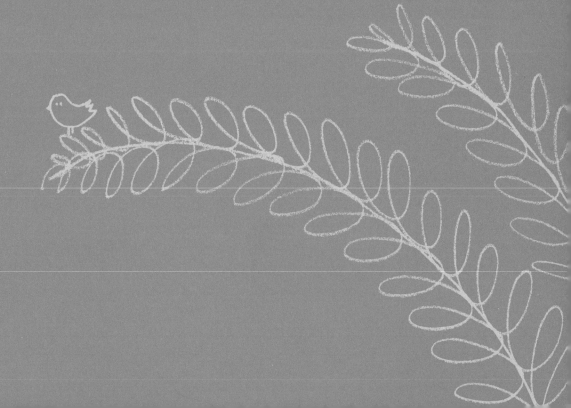

Babbit

For Ava
and Scarlett,

and Babbit,
of course.

EGMONT
We bring stories to life

First published in Great Britain 2011
by Egmont UK Limited
239 Kensington High Street
London W8 6SA

Text and illustrations copyright © Lydia Monks 2011
Lydia Monks has asserted her moral rights

ISBN 978 1405 2542 2 9 (Hardback)
ISBN 978 1405 2542 3 6 (Paperback)

1 3 5 7 9 10 8 6 4 2

A CIP catalogue record for this title
is available from the British Library

Printed and bound in Singapore

Written and Illustrated by **Lydia Monks**

Babbit

EGMONT

Hello! I'm Babbit.
I live here with
the Big One and
the Little One.

The Little One is supposed to look after me,
but she's not really very good at it.

Just look at what happened today . . .

We'd had a lovely picnic. Well, I say 'lovely' but there weren't quite enough carrots for my liking.

Anyway, we were just packing everything away, when

– lollopy lop ears –

I was grabbed!

Just like that.

And she didn't see!

Now, just **hang on** a moment!

Who had grabbed
my ears like that?
Very **rude,** if you ask me!

Ah! It was the **Witchy One.**

There's a **Snappy One** and
a **Growly One** and **Snorty One** too.
They are **always** playing tricks on us.
Jumping out at us and pulling faces.

They don't play nicely at all.
The **meanies!**

Don't panic, I thought.

The **Big One** and the **Little One** will be looking for me by now.

So, I waited and I waited,

and I waited . . .

. . . but they didn't come.

This wasn't funny any more. Not funny at all.
I had splinters in my bottom and that's not nice,
I can tell you!

'Let me go,' I squeaked as loudly as I could.

But Witchy, Snappy, Growly and Snorty
were too busy arguing to notice.

'I'm having his little fluffy tail,'
said the Witchy One.

'You can have his ears.'

'But ears taste yukky!' said the Growly One.

Wiggle my whiskers!
They weren't really going to eat me, were they?

I think a nice crunchy carrot would be
much tastier than little old me.

But wait! What was that?
It was them. The Big One and the Little One.

Boing de de boing boing!

At last! I was saved!

'Let's get out of here,' I whispered,

'before they eat the lot of us.'

The Little One untied me and we tiptoed away.

But then . . .

CRACK!

Oh no!

'Run, run, run!' I squealed.

And we ran.

Crunch, snap, *crunch!* We tore through the trees.

Whoosh, whee, *whoosh!* We leapt over logs.

Snap, scrunch, *snap.*

We legged it through the leaves.

They were nearly catching up.

Blinking bob tails!

Phew!

We'd lost them.

Thank our lucky lettuce leaves for that!

But what now?

Aaaarrgghh!

I was being p u l l e d

this way,

that way,

this way,

that way,

until . . .

. . . the Little One rescued me!

And bless my little bunny bottom,
that Little One can run. *Fast.*

We *ran* and *ran* and *ran*, and then . . .

BUMP!

We ran straight into
the Biggest One of All.

Oh, bless my blinking bob tail,
we were saved!

*Those others are in trouble now,
I thought. It's the naughty seats
for them, I bet!*

And I was right, you know!
That's what happens
when you don't play nicely.

And now, here I am,
tucked up in my favourite place.
Here, with the Little One, all snuggly.
Maybe tomorrow she will look after me a bit better.

I do hope so, don't you?

Night night! x

The End